W9-AMQ-280

Short Tales
CHINESE MYTHS

PANGU SEPARATES THE SKY FROM THE EARTH

A CHINESE CREATION MYTH

CHILDREN'S LIBRARY

ANITA YASUDA & JOK

magic wagon

visit us at www.abdopublishing.com

Printed in the United States of America, North Mankato, Minnesota.
102013
012014
 This book contains at least 10% recycled materials.

Adapted Text by Anita Yasuda
Illustrations by Jok
Edited by Stephanie Hedlund and Rochelle Baltzer
Interior Layout by Renée LaViolette

Library of Congress Cataloging-in-Publication Data

Yasuda, Anita.
  Pangu separates the sky from the earth : a Chinese creation myth / adapted by Anita Yasuda ; illustrated by Jok.
    pages cm. -- (Short tales Chinese myths)
  ISBN 978-1-62402-034-6
1. Tales--China--Juvenile literature. 2. Mythology, Chinese--Juvenile literature. 3. Creation--Folklore--Juvenile literature. I. Jok (Artist) illustrator. II. Title.
  GR335.Y3756 2014
  398.20931--dc23
                                                                2013025315

MYTHICAL CREATURES

PANGU

The creator of the
universe

YIN

A female force, shown by
the color black

YANG

A male force, shown by
the color white

Note: The Chinese names in this book use the pinyin
system to represent the Chinese language in English.

INTRODUCTION

Pangu Separates the Sky from the Earth tells the tale of a special being called Pangu. Pangu is said to have made the world and everything in it. In order for the world to take shape, Pangu must part the light called Yin from the dark called Yang. Yin and Yang have been important ideas in China since ancient times.

Xu Zheng was the first to record the myth *Pangu Separates the Sky from the Earth* in the third century CE. The story is found in his book *Sanwu Liji (Historical Records of the Three Sovereign Divinities and the Five Gods)*.

There are several variations of this creation myth. This version of the Pangu legend is adapted from material in D.A. Mackenzie's *Myths of China and Japan* printed in 1923. Mackenzie was a well-known Scottish journalist and author of many books on folklore.

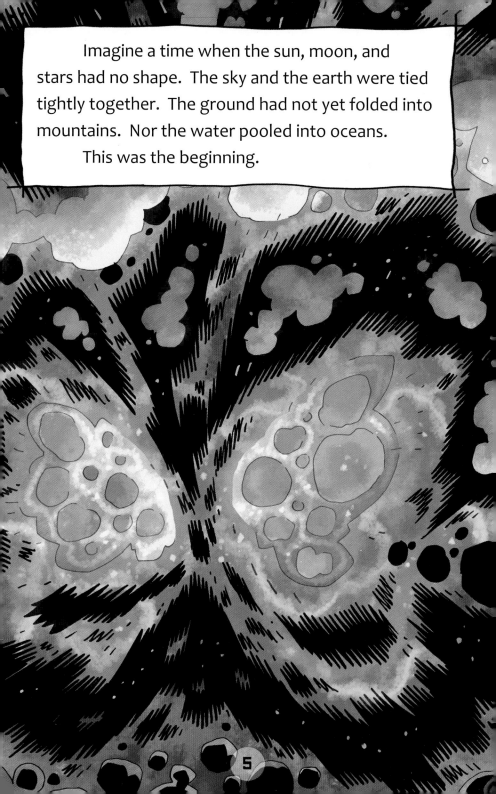

Imagine a time when the sun, moon, and stars had no shape. The sky and the earth were tied tightly together. The ground had not yet folded into mountains. Nor the water pooled into oceans.

This was the beginning.

Long ago, there was only light and dark. The light was called Yang. The dark was called Yin. One could not live without the other.

Light and dark swirled round and round.
They were trapped in a great egg.

Within the egg, light and dark were held together in a dance. They pulled and tugged at each other. They tumbled and spun for an eternity. It was chaos.

Then within the light and dark, the first being was born. The being's name was Pangu.

Pangu did not wake up. He stayed in the egg and slept. As Pangu slept, he grew bigger and bigger.

After 18,000 years, Pangu woke up. He was now a towering giant. Two horns grew out of his head. In one hand he held a hammer and in the other a chisel.

Pangu was the only being in the universe. He looked around with wonder at the swirling light and dark cloud. Chaos was not calm like his sleep had been.

"I will make something out of this confusion," Pangu said.

Pangu took his great hammer. Raising it high above his head, he swung it at the egg over and over again.

Pangu worked for a very long time. Sweat dripped from his body. His muscles strained. Pangu grew tired. Yet he did not stop.

Then one day chaos opened. The light and the dark split in two. What a sight Pangu saw as light floated upward. It became the blue sky. Dark was heavier. It became the earth.

Though Pangu had parted the light from the dark, he could not rest.

"I do not want the sky and the earth to ever join again," said Pangu. Pangu worried that chaos might return if this happened.

So he used all his strength to push the sky up
with his hands. His feet pushed on the earth below.

Pangu stood like a mighty pillar holding up the sky. Each day, he grew taller and taller. And each day, he pushed the sky higher and higher.

Pangu remained between the sky and earth for 18,000 years. It was a long, hard job.

"I will stand between the sky and earth," said Pangu, "so that they never join again."

When Pangu thought he could do this no more, the sky and earth no longer needed him.

"The sky can rise no more," Pangu said. "The earth can sink no lower."

Pangu gazed at the sky and earth. He was very pleased.

"Now, all is peaceful," Pangu said.

At last Pangu could lie down and rest. He was now very tired. Pangu stretched his body over the earth and slept.

Pangu's sleep deepened until he could no longer wake. Then, something amazing happened. Everything on the earth and in the sky began to take shape.

Pangu's arms and legs became the four directions—north, south, east, and west. His body turned into rich soil and lush fields.

Pangu's head formed mountains. These rose high above the ground. His bones and teeth changed into precious stones.

The blood in Pangu's veins became the rushing rivers and vast oceans. His sweat changed into rain. His tears became the morning dew.

The hair on Pangu's body turned into beautiful flowers, plants, and trees. It spread around the earth like a green carpet.

Pangu's voice became the deep sound of thunder. His breath made the clouds in the sky and the wind that blows over the land.

28

Pangu's right eye became the moon. It floated into the sky. His left eye became the sun. It joined the moon in the heavens.

Millions of lights rushed from Pangu's beard. They arranged themselves in the sky. These became the twinkling stars.

Pangu's body was almost gone, but he had one last gift to give. Under Pangu's sky filled with light, the first people were born. There was now life from the lowest valleys to the highest mountains. All was good.

And now you know how Pangu created the world and everything in it. When you wake in the morning and say good night to the moon, think of Pangu.